This book is dedicated to all the farm and ranch wives who have to put up with noisy kids, ornery husbands, and sorry dogs.

Maverick Books
Published by Gulf Publishing Company
P.O. Box 2608 Houston, Texas 77252-2608

C D E F G H

Second Printing, November, 1990

Library of Congress Cataloging-in-Publication Data

Erickson, John R., 1943–
The case of the one-eyed killer stud horse / John R. Erickson: illustrations by Gerald L. Holmes.
p. cm.
At head of title: Hank the Cowdog.
"The eighth exciting adventure in the Hank the Cowdog series".
Summary: Hank the cowdog goes to the rescue as a wild, one-eyed horse creates havoc on the ranch but some of his outrageous stunts get him into more trouble than he bargained for.
ISBN 0-87719-144-1 (pbk.).—ISBN 0-87719-145-X (hbk.).—ISBN 0-87719-146-8 (cassette)
1. Dogs—Fiction. [1. Dogs—Fiction. 2. Mystery and detective stories. 3. Humorous stories. 4. West (U.S.)—Fiction.] I. Holmes, Gerald L., ill. II. Title.
PS3555.R428H287 1990
813'.54—dc20 90-13571
[Fic] CIP
AC

Printed in the United States of America.

THE CASE OF THE ONE-EYED KILLER STUD HORSE

· John R. Erickson ·

Illustrations by Gerald L. Holmes

Maverick Books
Published by Gulf Publishing Company
Houston, Texas

Contents

Have you read all of Hank's adventures?
Now available in paperback at $6.95:

		ISBN
1	Hank the Cowdog	0-87719-130-1
2	The Further Adventures of Hank the Cowdog	0-87719-117-4
3	It's a Dog's Life	0-87719-128-X
4	Murder in the Middle Pasture	0-87719-133-6
5	Faded Love	0-87719-136-0
6	Let Sleeping Dogs Lie	0-87719-138-7
7	The Curse of the Incredible Priceless Corncob	0-87719-141-7
8	The Case of the One-Eyed Killer Stud Horse	0-87719-144-1
9	The Case of the Halloween Ghost	0-87719-147-6
10	Every Dog Has His Day	0-87719-150-6
11	Lost in the Dark Unchanted Forest	0-87719-118-2
12	The Case of the Fiddle-Playing Fox	0-87719-170-0
13	The Wounded Buzzard on Christmas Eve	0-87719-175-1
14	Monkey Business	0-87719-180-8
15	The Case of the Missing Cat	0-87719-185-9
16	Lost in the Blinding Blizzard	0-87719-192-1

All books are available on audio cassette too! ($15.95 for two cassettes)

Also available on cassettes: Hank the Cowdog's Greatest Hits!

Volume 1 ISBN 0-916941-20-5 $6.95
Volume 2 ISBN 0-916941-37-X $6.95
Volume 3 ISBN 0-87719-194-8 $6.95

CHAPTER

1

THE CASE OF THE CODED TRANSMISSION

It's me again, Hank the Cowdog. Fall is a beautiful time of the year in the Texas Panhandle, or so I thought before the relatives descended upon the ranch for the Thanksgiving holidays and Sally May went lame in her right leg and I found myself involved in the Case of the One-eyed Killer Stud Horse.

Sounds pretty exciting, huh? Just wait until you meet Tuerto, the One-eyed Killer Stud Horse. He'll scare the children so bad, they'll have to sleep with their mothers and dads for a whole week. They'll see his gotch eye in their dreams, and if they're not careful, they're liable to wet the bed.

Any of you kids who wet the bed, don't mention my name. Don't mention *your* name either. Just pretend it didn't happen. When Mom and Dad wake up in the night and find that big cold wet spot in the middle of the bed, tell 'em that it rained during the night and the roof leaked.

Where was I? Under the gas tanks, one of my favorite spots on the ranch and the place where many of my adventures seem to begin. Drover and I were asleep on our gunny sack beds, having returned at daylight from our patrols around the ranch.

Little did we know what adventures lay in store for us because we were catching a few winks of sleep after putting in a long night of patrol work. I've already said that, but it doesn't hurt to repeat yourself repeat yourself once in a while in a while.

I love to sleep. Sometimes I dream about bones and long juicy strips of steak fat. I remember one dream in particular when Sally May drove up to the gas tanks and unloaded a strip of steak fat that was half a mile long. That was a dream to remember. It took me two weeks to eat that strip of steak fat. When I was done, I couldn't walk. Had to crawl around on all-fours with a roller skate under my belly.

That was one of my all-time great dreams. Another involved a fifty foot steak bone, I mean a bone as big as a tree. Took me a month and a half to eat that rascal. After I'd finished, I was telling Drover about how I'd just by George destroyed a steak bone that looked like a tree.

He gave me his usual stupid expression and said, "You mean you ate that tree that looked like a steak bone?"

I didn't pay any attention to him, but I spent the next three months sneezing sawdust, which made me wonder. That was all in a dream, of course.

Bone-dreams and steakfat-dreams are wonderful, but perhaps the wonderfulest dreams of all are the ones that star Beulah the Collie.

Ah, Sweet Beulah! Be still my heart! Return to thy cage of ribs and venture not forth into the dark night of darkness like a stalking jungle beast venturing and stalking through the inky dark blackness of . . . something. Love, I guess.

Mercy. Just the thought of that woman gets me in an uproar. Just mention her name and suddenly the same mouth that reduces trees to sawdust and pulverizes monsters begins gushing poetry. Beats anything I ever saw.

Experts will tell you that I'm a very lucky dog. I mean, it ain't every dog that has the honor of falling in love with the most beautiful collie gal in the whole entire world. Even more experts would tell you how lucky SHE is.

Boy, is she lucky, but sometimes I wonder if she knows it. She keeps showing up with that birddog. I just don't understand . . . oh well. In my dreams she belongs to me. I don't allow birddogs into my dreams.

Anyways, me and Drover were under the gas tanks, melted and molded into our gunny sacks, and throwing up long lines of Z's, when all of a sudden I heard Drover say, "Zebras wear pajamas but you can't spot a leopard with a spyglass."

Without opening my eyes or bringing myself to the Full Alert Mode, I ran that statement through my data banks. All at once, it didn't make sense, so I lifted one ear to intercept any other transmissions, shall we say, from my pipsqueak assistant. Sure enough, I picked up another.

"There's no pullybones in a chicken sandwich."

This one made me suspicious, so I opened one eye. Drover appeared to be 100% asleep, yet he continued to transmit messages in a code I had never run across before. I listened.

"If you take the dog out of doggerel, the

motor won't start without peanut butter."

Ah ha! A certain pattern began to emerge. I opened both eyes, cranked myself up to a sitting position, and listened more carefully. What I had originally taken to be the incoherent ramblings of Drover's so-called mind were showing signs of being something else—perhaps coded messages from some magic source?

How else could you explain Drover's use of a big word like "doggerel?" Or his reference to zebras and leopards and auto mechanics? I knew for a fact that Drover had never seen a zebra or a leopard, and I had reason to suspect that he didn't know peanuts about starting motors.

Your ordinary dog would have dismissed it all as nonsense and gone back to sleep, but as you might have already surmised, I decided to probe this thing a little deeper. I moved closer and listened. He spoke again.

"When the sun rises in the morning in the east, the biscuits rise in the oven in the yeast."

Hmm, yes. This message not only rhymed, but it also hinted at some deep, profoundical meaning. This transmission had to be originating from some mysterious source outside of Drover.

I decided to draw him out with a clever line of questions. It was risky. I mean, the sound of my voice might very well wake him up and spoil everything, but that was a risk I had to take.

What we had here was The Case of the Coded Transmission, and at last the clues were beginning to fall into place. Your ordinary dogs, your poodles and your cheewahwahs and your cocker spaniels, would miss all of the important stuff. I mean, it would go right over their heads like a duck out of water.

So there I was, sifting clues and finding patterns and preparing clever questions that would draw even more startling revelations from the mind of my sleeping assistant. As I said, it was a risky procedure but I had to give it a try.

"All right, Drover. You hear my voice, is that correct?"

"Mumbo jumbo."

"Does that mean 'yes' in your secret code?"

"Jumbo mumbo."

"Are you trying to reverse the code on me now?"

"Mumbo hocus pocus."

"What happened to jumbo?"

"Jumbo hocus pocus."

"Thought you could fool me, didn't you? You should have known better. As I've often said, Drover, it isn't the size of the dog in the fight that matters. It's the size of the fog in the dog."

"Foggy doggy mumbo jumbo."

"Exactly. I've locked into your code now. You can hear my voice, Drover, and you

will do exactly as I say. You will answer my questions . . ."

"Gargle murgle guttersnipe."

". . . but not until I ask them. Stand by for the first question. Ready? Mark! Here is the first question: Give me the full name of the mysterious source of these messages."

"Mumble grumble mutter."

"You're muttering, Drover, I can't understand what you're saying."

"Mumble grumble rumble."

"That's better. Is that the full name of the mysterious source of these messages?"

"Murgle gurgle snore zzzzzzz."

"Hmmm. Obviously he's not from around here. That's a foreign name if I ever heard one. Any name with that many Z's in it is bound to be foreign."

"Chicken feather jelly."

"What? Repeat that message and concentrate on your diction."

"Dictionary jelly murgle snore."

"That's better. All right, Drover, this brings us to our last and most important question, to the darkness behind the veil, so to speak. What is the evil purpose behind these coded messages sent to you from the mysterious foreign source?"

I held my breath and waited. Suddenly, the screen door slammed up at the house. Drover leaped to his feet. His eyes popped open, revealing . . .

Very little, actually. His ears were crooked, his eyes were crossed. He staggered two steps to the left and two steps to the right.

"Scraps!" he said in a squeaky voice.

"What? Is that the evil purpose of all these messages?"

"What are you talking about?"

"You know exactly what I'm talking about. Answer the question."

"Sally May just came out of the house. I bet she's got some scraps from breakfast."

"Huh?" At last it all fit together. "You're exactly right, Drover. And speaking of evil purposes, unless we do some fancy stepping, the cat will beat us to the scraps. Come on, Drover, to the yard gate!"

And so it was that, having solved The Case of the Coded Transmission, we turned to more serious business—delivering Pete the Barncat his first defeat of the day.

CHAPTER

2

STRICKEN WITH SNEEZAROMA BECAUSE SHE WHACKED ME ON THE NOSE WITH A WOODEN SPOON

We went streaking up the hill, with me in the lead and Drover bringing up the rear. When we got to the yard gate, I glanced around and saw that we had succeeded in our first objective.

Sally May and Loper were there talking, but Pete was nowhere in sight. Ha ha, ho ho! In her right hand, Sally May held a plate, in her left a wooden spoon.

I turned to my assistant and gave him a worldly smile. "This is going to be a piece of cake, Drover."

"Oh boy! Usually it's burned toast and a busted egg."

"What?"

"I said, usually it's burned toast . . ."

"I heard that, Drover, but it shows that you misunderstood what I said."

"Oh."

" 'Piece of cake' is an expression, a figure of speech. It means, 'This is going to be easy.' "

"Oh. Well, that's easy enough."

"Exactly. You see, Drover, sometimes our words have subtle meanings that go beyond the actual words. That's the beauty of language, its many shades of meaning."

"Yeah, and on a hot day that shade sure comes in handy."

"Exactly. So there you are, son, a little lesson in the endless variety of language."

"It's pretty good, all right. Sure hope it's chocolate."

"What?"

"I've never had chocolate cake in the morning."

For a moment I considered giving the runt a tongue lashing, but just then Loper spoke up.

"Hon, I'm going over to check that fence between us and Billy's west pasture. His stud horse got through the fence yesterday and I found him in the home pasture. I don't want that crazy thing coming up around the house. He could hurt someone."

"Oh my!"

"He's got a mean streak and only one eye. I wouldn't want to take any chances with you or Little Alfred. He's kind of dangerous."

Loper turned his eyes on me. I gave him a big smile and wagged my tail and went over and jumped up on him. Licked him on the hand too. I wanted to build up a few Loyal Dog Points, see. In this line of work, a guy needs to get points in the bank any time he can.

Anyways, I jumped up on Loper, said howdy, wished him good morning, and, you know, let him know that I was there on the job. He looked down into my face, curled his lip, and pushed me away.

"Get down! You stink."

HUH? Well, I . . .

"If we had a dog on this ranch that was worth anything," he wiped his hand on his jeans, "we wouldn't have to worry about Billy's stud horse. Anyway, when the cousins get here, don't let them play in the pasture."

"All right. They'll be here around eleven. Will you be home for lunch?"

"I don't know. I've got to help the neighbors move some cattle around. I might be late getting home."

While they were talking, Sally May held the plate about waist-high. I got kind of curious as to what tasty morsels might be on it, so I hopped up on my back legs and took a peek.

Hmmm. Scrambled eggs, five or six fatty ends of bacon, and two pieces of burned toast. Burned toast must have been one of Sally May's specialties, because she seemed to crank out two or three pieces of it every morning.

I'm not too crazy about burned toast, but fatty ends of bacon . . . I can get worked up over fatty ends of bacon.

Sally May had got herself caught up in a conversation and had forgotten to scrape our goodies out on the ground, is what had happened, and it suddenly occurred to me that that plate was probably getting pretty heavy.

I mean, you don't think about fatty ends of bacon weighing very much, but you take enough of them and put them together and you'll come up with a whole entire hog that might weigh, oh, three-four hundred pounds. (That's where bacon comes from, don't you know. Hogs. Big hogs.)

Now, Sally May was a tough old gal but she

had her limits. I'd seen her bucking bales of alfalfa on the hay wagon and I'd seen her carrying sacks of chicken feed from her car into the machine shed, but I'd never seen her lift a three hundred pound hog. Even Loper couldn't do that.

She had no business lifting hogs. I mean, here was the mother of a small child. Didn't she have enough to do, keeping up the house and the garden and the chickens, caring for a child and a husband? Seemed to me it was my duty to lighten her load a little bit.

I've always figgered that one of the reasons we're put here on this earth is to help others. That's why, when I have a chance to ease someone else's burden, I try to do it.

And let me tell you, it wasn't an easy thing to do. I mean, there I was standing on my back legs, and I had to turn my head to the side, ease my nose over the edge of the plate, and snag the bacon ends with my tongue.

You ever try to snag something with your tongue, when your head's turned sideways? It sounds easy, but you can take my word for it, it ain't. I'm not sure why. A guy's tongue ought to work just as well sideways as up and down. I mean, why should a tongue care which way is up and which is down?

Beats me, but the point is that it was a difficult maneuver. No ordinary dog would have even attempted it. I not only attempted it but came *that close* to pulling it off. Here's how I did it. (You might want to jot down a few notes.)

First, I extended my tongue to its fully-extended position, at which point I had something like six inches of powerful tongue reeled out of my mouth. Second, I concentrated all my powers of concentration on putting a curl into the end of it.

Pretty tough.

Thirdly, with the same curl in the end of the same tongue we have been discussing, I began easing a bacon end over toward the edge of the plate, even though the root of my tongue was getting tired from the strain of being fully extended. (Try it and see if the root of your tongue doesn't get tired.)

Fourthly, just as I was about to throw a coil of tongue around the juicy end of bacon fat, reel it back into my mouth, and gobble it down, Sally May saw what I was doing and smacked me on the nose with the wooden spoon.

"Get down, Hank! I'll feed you when Pete gets here."

In other words, she had misinterpreted my intentions. Maybe she thought I was merely trying to steal the bacon before her stupid and greedy cat arrived to hog it all. Not a bad idea, actually, but of course I had higher motives.

On this outfit, it seems to be all right for a cat to be a hog, but let a dog try to be a hog just once and WHACK! He gets it across the nose with a wooden spoon.

It ain't fair, but let's don't get started on that.

I turned to Drover. "What are you grinning about?"

"Who me?"

"I saw that silly grin on your face. I'd advise you to wipe it off before . . ."

That whack on the nose had a strange effect on me, made me sneeze. I'm not talking about one little sneeze or even two, I'm talking about a bunch of BIG ones, all in a row, one after another, bang-bang-bang—or sneeze-sneeze-sneeze, you might say. And each one of them sneezes just about blew the end of my nose off.

This is a fairly rare medical condition known as "Sneezaroma." Those who get it never forget it, because you can't stop sneezing.

Drover still had that silly grin on his face.

"Bless you."

"Thank you."

"You're welcome. You got hay fever?"

"No, I don't have ACHOOOO! Hay fever."

"Bless you."

"Thank you."

"You're welcome. Sure sounds like hay fever to me."

"Sounds can be deceiving, son. Just because I sneeze, that doesn't mean I have ACHOOOO!"

"Bless you. I have hay fever too, so I know how it feels."

"I just told you, Numbskull, I *don't have hay fever.* Sally May hit me on the nose with a spoon and it gave me Sneezaroma. Let's ACHOO drop it."

"Bless you."

"Thank you."

"You're welcome. Maybe you're allergic to spoons. ACHOO! Gosh, maybe I'm allergic to your sneezes."

"Bless you."

"Thanks, Hank."

"You're welcome. No, I don't think so, Drover. More than likely it's just ACHOO!"

"Bless you."

"Thank you."

"You're welcome. ACHOO!"
"Bless you."
"Thanks, Hank."
"You're ACHOO!"
"Bless ACHOO!"

"Thank you, and bless you ACHOO!"

"ACHOOO!"

"ACHOOO!"

We were getting nowhere fast. Carrying on an intelligent conversation with Drover is hard enough under the best of conditions, but when we're both sneezing, it's very near impossible.

I was all set to head back down to the gas tanks and put my poor nose to bed, when all at once I saw something that made the hair stand up on the back of my neck. Prancing down the hill from the machine shed was one of my least favorite characters on the ranch—my arch-enemy, to be exact.

Pete the Barncat.

He had his stupid tail stuck straight up in the air and he was purring like a little motorboat. No doubt he was coming to hog all the breakfast scraps, but it was my job to see that he failed in his mission of greed.

"Hold up, Drover. Unless I'm badly mistaken, we're fixing to get ourselves into some combat. We've got a cat coming in at two o'clock."

"Well, better late than tardy."

"Exactly. Battle stations, Drover, and prepare for some heavy duty barking!"

"AAAA-CHOOOO!"

"That's not barking."

"I'm sorry."

"You're welcome."

"Thanks, Hank."

And with that, we turned our menacing glares on Pete the Barncat.

CHAPTER 3

THE CASE OF THE EMBEZZLED SCRAMBLED EGGS

I've never understood exactly what it is about Pete that gets me so stirred up. Under ordinary circumstances, I keep an iron grip on my emotions, which comes in handy in the security business because emotions have no place in that spear.

Sphere, I probably should say. I don't like Pete, that's the point. He's your typical arrogant, sniveling, scheming, insolent cat. I don't like the way he holds his tail, the way he walks, or the way he rubs up against everything in sight.

I don't like his face. I don't like his whiney voice. I don't like his attitude. I don't like cats, but I wouldn't like Pete even if he wasn't a cat.

When he appeared on the scene, my ears jumped up and a growl began to rumble deep in my throat. It was just by George automatic.

By this time, Loper had left in his pickup, but Sally May was still there with her plate of goodies, which I had every intention of protecting from Pete. Sally May must have heard me growling.

"Hank, stop that! I won't have you bullying the cat."

I twisted my head around and looked up at her with my most sincere expression of sincerity. Bullying the cat! I hadn't even touched the little snot, much less given him the pounding he so richly deserved.

I whimpered and whapped my tail on the ground.

She bent down and brought her face only inches away from the end of my nose. "I know what you're thinking, Hank, but if you start tormenting the cat again, I'm going to whack you over the head with this spoon."

Suddenly I was seized by an impulse to lick her on the nose. I don't know why. It just seemed the appropriate thing to do. My tongue shot out and gave her a big, loving, juicy, peace-making, forgiving, friendly cowdog lick on the nose.

And it was such a big extra special lick that some of it lapped over and got her on the mouth.

My goodness. You'd have thought that she'd been bitten by a water moccasin, the way she drew back and stiffened up.

"Don't do that! I don't like dogs who lick all the time! No, no, no. *Don't lick.*"

And here's the real shocker. She not only wiped her mouth with the back of her hand, but she *spit.* Or is it "spitted?" "Spat?" She spatted, not at anyone in particular but in a way that made you think she'd just gotten a taste of poison.

Really shocked me. I mean, all those years I'd thought she was a proper lady, and then to see her spitting . . . well, it kind of disappointed me, I guess you'd say. I'd expected more from Sally May than spitting.

I turned to Drover and shrugged. "How do you please these people? They don't want you to growl, they don't want you to bark, they don't want you to hamburgerize the cats. After years and years of working up the courage to show a little affection, you give 'em a lick on the face and, whammo, they throw it right back at you."

"Maybe she doesn't like dogs."

"And once you've been rebuked and rejected and scorned, you withdraw into the inner recessitudes of your dark self, and something happens to you, Drover. A guy begins to change in little ways. It makes him hard and cold and hard."

"You said 'hard' twice."

"It makes him think about running away and becoming an outlaw, a killer dog who howls in the night and spends his life looking for revenge."

"I spent all day looking for a bone once."

"Exactly. Yes, rejection is a terrible thing, Drover."

"I guess so. Maybe you'd better not lick her in the face any more."

I stared at the runt. "Is that all you can say? Is that all the comfort you can give me in this time of sorrow?"

"Well . . . you might try it and see if it helps."

"A simple answer from a simple mind. I should have known better than to expose the burning embers of my heart to the likes of you."

"Heartburn's pretty bad, but it beats hay fever."

At that moment, I realized that Pete was rubbing against my right front leg and flicking the end of his tail across my chin. Suddenly, I forgot my sorrows and began thinking nasty thoughts.

"Hi, Hankie. Sure is a pretty day, isn't it?"

My lips curled, my eyes flared, and a growl rumbled in my throat. I glanced up at Sally May. Had she been looking the other way, Pete wouldn't have thought the day was so pretty. But she wasn't looking the other way. She was looking at me.

"Don't you dare! Now, you dogs had better learn to get along with the cat. Here, kitty kitty."

Pete gave me one last grin, stepped on my tail, and shot through a hole in the fence. Then, before my very eyes, Sally May scraped MY juicy, fatty bacon ends out on the ground and gave them all to the cat.

Well, hey, that was too much. I barked. I howled. I cried and moaned and protested this injustice. Sally May came over to the fence and gave me a scowl.

"Oh be quiet, Hank. I've got some for you too. Here." She scraped something off the plate. It hit the ground.

I sniffed it. Scrambled eggs and burned toast. I gave her a mournful look and whapped my tail. I mean, scrambled eggs are okay, but I had sort of prepared my taste buds for something in the bacon department.

I put some serious begs on her. No sale. All right, if scrambled eggs was the best we could do . . . I looked down and was stunned to see that the eggs had vanished. I turned to Drover, who was licking his chops.

"Did you eat my eggs?"

"Who me?"

"Of course you did. Yes, it's all coming clear now. First the cat steals my bacon, then my own trusted assistant embezzles my eggs. Oh vile world! Oh wickedness! Oh treachery! How much deeper canst thou sink?"

"Are you asking me or the world?"

"I'm asking you, Mr. Egg Embezzler."

"Oh. What was the question again?"

Funny, I couldn't remember the question either. Oh well. "The point is, you should be ashamed of yourself. For that, Drover, you can spend the next hour standing in the corner."

"Oh drat."

"Don't argue with me. Go to your room, put your nose in the corner, and say the following five hundred times: 'Only a chicken would steal an egg from his friend.' "

"Only a chicken . . . gosh, Hank, what if I can't remember all that?"

"This afternoon, I'll give you a test to make sure you memorized it. If you flunk, then you will have crossed over the line between Serious Trouble and Very Serious Trouble. I wouldn't want to speculate on the consequences of that."

"Oh darn. Well, if I admit I ate your eggs, would you let me off without any punishment?"

"Negative. There's no plea bargaining on this ranch—not while I'm in charge and not when I've been looted by my own employees. Now go, and shame on you for a whole hour."

Drover hung his head and went padding down to the gas tanks. I watched the little mutt and hoped the punishment wasn't too severe. I only wanted to break his bad habits, not his spirit.

There are times, up here at the top, when a guy is tempted to soften his position on crime and punishment. But part of being a cowdog and a Head of Ranch Security lies in being just a little tougher than your average run of dogs.

Drover was the one with egg on his face, and now the foot was on the other shoe.

CHAPTER

4

BACON GREASE OVER BURNED TOAST MAKES A LOUSY BREAKFAST

Once Drover had left to go serve his time in jail, I turned my attention back to the scene before me.

There was Greedygut the Cat, eating my juicy bacon ends. As you may know, cats don't have a real good set of chewing teeth. Their teeth are more like spikes or needles—better for inflicting pain on innocent children than the teeth of a dog, but not as good for crushing bones or chewing meat.

In other words, I still had some hope that Pete would choke on my bacon. Stranger things have happened in this old world. If you've ever watched a cat eating, you know that they often yowl while they chew. Also, they don't chew their food twenty-one times. They'll hit it four, five, or six times, then try to swaller it whole—yowling and growling at the same time.

And sometimes they choke.

I didn't wish Pete any bad luck, but if he had strangled himself on my bacon, he would have improved the world and served the cause of justice—also saved some juicy bacon ends for certain observers whose names we don't need to mention.

I waited and watched and hoped. The longer I waited and watched and hoped, the more I began to realize that this would not be a lucky day for the ranch, for the cat devoured my breakfast and didn't choke.

At that point in my career, I began looking around for secondary options, such as the two pieces of burned toast lying on the ground before me. I sniffed them. I took one of them in my mouth and gummed it around before spitting it out.

Whether you gum it or chew it or sniff it, burned toast remains basically burned toast.

But just then, I saw Sally May come out of the house with an orange juice can in her hand. She walked past the cat, who was now licking his hind leg with long strokes of his tongue, and proceeded to the south corner of the fence. She leaned across the fence and poured the contents of the orange juice can out on the ground.

Hmm. Why would Sally May be pouring orange juice out on the ground? That didn't make sense. Something strange was going on here, and I needed to check it out.

I went slipping down the fence. Sally May saw me. I stopped.

"No, Hank. It's just bacon grease. It's messy, and it'll make you sick if you eat it. Now go on."

Oh. Bacon grease. Hmm, yes. I could smell it now. Smelled pretty good. Smelled VERY good. Bacon grease may not be exactly the same as bacon, but at a distance one smells about as good as another.

I waited for Sally May to go back into the house. Little Alfred had come out by then and she told him not to get dirty because the kinfolks would be arriving in an hour. Then she went inside.

I slipped back to the spot where I had left the two pieces of charred toast, picked one up in my enormous jaws, glanced around to make sure Sally May wasn't looking, and made my

G. L. Holmes

way south down the fence. The further I went, the stronger that bacon smell became. By the time I reached the spot, I could almost taste it.

Now, it didn't look all that great, I'll have to admit that. When you pour cold bacon grease out on the ground, it looks like something you wouldn't want to eat. But the aroma . . . that's the important thing. Looks ain't everything in this old world.

See, I had worked out this very clever strategy in my mind. Listen to this. If a guy is denied real bacon and is left with nothing to eat but burned toast, he can sop the toast in the grease. While making efficient use of the resources at hand, he also fools his taste buds by making them think he's eating bacon, see.

Pretty shrewd. No cat in history has ever come up with a plan that good.

Well, I took one last glance around to make sure that the, uh, Kitchen Police weren't watching, then I dropped the toast right into the middle of the brown blob . . . into the bacon grease, I should say. I oozed it around, flipped it over, and let the other side soak up . . .

You know, that stuff smelled so wonderful that my mouth began to water. It's hard to express a dog's deep yearning for bacon. I couldn't remember the last time I'd experienced the savage delight of gobbling bacon, nor could I remember a single time in my long and glorious career when I had had at my disposal all the bacon I wanted or could eat.

I postponed the first bite as long as I could. I mean, that's part of the fun of eating—knowing you've got the goodies there in front of you but forbidding yourself from diving into it.

I sniffed it. I licked my chops. I drooled over it. I rehearsed that first bite over and over in my mind. I was just about ready to begin the procedure when I heard a voice.

"You'd better not eat that bacon grease, Hankie. It'll make you sick."

That was Pete. He was sitting on the other side of the fence, purring, twitching the end of his tail, and staring at me with his big cattish eyes.

"Oh yeah? Who says?"

"Me. And Sally May."

"Sally May's opinion carried some weight around here until you started quoting her, and that just about ruined it."

"Truth is truth, Hankie, regardless of who says it."

"Oh yeah? Well, I've got one better for you.

Truth is truth until it comes from the mouth of a cat. There's no truth so true that a cat can't twist it into a falsehood."

He blinked and smiled. "Well, if I felt that way about it, Hankie, I'd eat all that bacon grease."

"Would you? That's very interesting, cat, because that's just what I'm fixing to do." I chuckled and gave him a wink. "You see, kitty-kitty, I understand your little scheme. You think I'll do the opposite of anything you say, right? You tell me to eat all the bacon grease, I eat none of it, I walk away and leave it all for you, right?"

"I was just trying to be helpful, Hankie."

"Oh Pete, it hurts me to see you slipping. This game of yours is old and tired. I mean, okay, maybe it worked once or twice, but that was years ago. Life goes on, cat. You can't toot your own horn if you've only got one string on your fiddle."

"You're mixing your metaphors, Hankie."

"No, I'm mixing business with pleasure. It's my business to beat you at your own shabby games, and it's a pleasure to do it. Now, if you'll just stand back and observe, I'll begin the procedure. Before your very eyes, you'll see me devour the toast in three bites, then lick up the remaining grease until nothing remains, not even a spot."

"You'll get sick."

I laughed in his face. "You're about to see one of the most experienced pot-lickers in Ochiltree County do his stuff. I mean, what I don't know about pot-licking hasn't even been tried yet, so stand back and study your lessons. Ready? Aim! Bonzai!"

I dived into the middle of that piece of toast. The procedure went off without a hitch. Within seconds, I had that piece of toast reduced to molecules (those are the basic building blocks of the universe, if you'd care to make a note of it), and true to my prediction, I did it in three bites.

Pete watched in sheer amazement. I'm sure he had never seen such an exhibition of brute skill.

I must admit that swallering the molecules of toast turned out to be no ball of wax, for some of the molecules still had the texture of burned toast. In other words, they scraped and scratched on the way down. But a little scraping and scratching has never scared me away from a good meal.

Upon completion of Step One of the procedure, I entered into Step Two. True to my prediction once again, I completely demolished the glob of bacon grease on the ground, licked it to the bare dirt and even managed to get some of the bare dirt in with the grease, can't say it tasted so good, I've never cared much for dirt, but what the heck, there's a price for everything.

The entire procedure, including Steps One and Two, required something less than one minute. I turned to Pete and gave him a smirk.

"What do you say now, cat? How does it feel to lose a big one?"

Before he could answer, Little Alfred, age three years and some odd months, came up behind him, grabbed him by the tail and made a wagon of him. Or maybe it was a plow, since Pete had his front claws out and did a pretty impressive job of plowing up the yard as he was being dragged around.

Little Alfred is hard on cats. That's one thing I've always admired about him. Fine kid, that Alfred.

Well, this was an unexpected pleasure. It isn't often that I can take time out of my busy schedule and watch someone else tormenting the cat. I drifted over to the yard gate, where I had a good view, and sat down to watch the show.

I loved it. You should have seen Pete's eyes. And his ears, yes, that was delicious too, had 'em pinned down and he was yowling and scowling and . . .

I burped. It just kind of snuck out.

Anyways, there was Little Alfred making the sounds of a tractor and pulling his cat-plow across the . . .

I burped again. Also noticed an unusual feeling in my, well, in the region between my lower ribs and . . . in the vicinity of my stomach, you might say, and . . . you know, all at once I didn't feel like a million dollars. It was closer to $9.95.

Anyways, Little Alfred and Pete plowed up the south side of the yard, and all at once I didn't feel worth a flip. I could hear some kind of strange noise coming from my innards—pretty muchly the sound you'd expect if you'd just eaten a couple of panthers and they'd started fighting. 'Course, I hadn't eaten any wildcats, only . . .

All at once the thought of bacon was less exciting than I'd ever thought possible. In fact, I decided that . . . I didn't want to think about bacon at that particular moment, and maybe never again for the rest of my life.

I didn't want to smell bacon either, but the

smell of bacon filled my nostrils. Oozy, drippy, greasy, smelly, stinky, oily bacon. Yuck!

I never did care much for bacon. It's too greasy for me. And once you get some stinky bacon grease on the hairs around your mouth, the smell stays with you and all you can smell is bacon, and I can't stand the smell of greasy, oily . . .

Right then and there, I took a solemn oath never to eat bacon again, nor bacon grease, nor burned toast, nor dirt. In fact, I took a solemn oath never to eat *anything* again, ever.

Fellers, I was sick, and I mean SICK. If the Angel of Death had come calling for me at that moment, I would have either jumped into his arms or throwed up, I couldn't tell which.

CHAPTER 5

WAS IT MY FAULT THAT SHE TRIPPED OVER ME AND TWISTED HER DADGUM ANKLE?

It was a real pity that I got sick at that particular moment, because the show in the back yard got better and better.

After using Pete for a plow, Little Alfred turned on the water hose and started irrigating him. I guess you know about cats and water. They don't get along. Old Pete had his ears pinned down, had a disgusted look on his face, and he was making a sound like a police siren.

On a better day, I would have considered this good wholesome entertainment. On a better day, I would have had something besides bacon on my mind. But this wasn't a better day.

I curled up in a ball in front of the yard gate and tried to think of anything but food. I tried it all—birds, rainbows, butterflies, pretty flowers. No luck. They all came out smelling like bacon grease.

Well, whilst I was there, listening to the cement mixer in my stomach, the back door burst open and Sally May came out, her housecoat flying in the breeze and the west side of her hair up in pink curlers.

"Alfred, oh Alfred! You're covered with mud and shame on you for being mean to the cat, and the company's going to be here any minute and the water pump quit working and we don't have any water pressure and I can't clean your daddy's ring around the bathtub and here you are wasting water and being mean to the cat!"

She marched over to my little pal and gave him a swat on the behind. He squalled. Then she bent over to rescue her waterlogged pet, and he being your typical dumb, ungrateful cat, hissed and scratched her, so she booted him across the yard and called him a name I'd never heard before.

Judging by the tone of her voice, I would

G.L. Holmes

guess that meant something besides Sweetie Pie.

It was a good kick too. When she got riled, old Sally May could be dangerous. Not only could she throw a rock, but she made a pretty good hand at booting cats. I was impressed—also glad that I was outside the yard and out of her range.

Well, she was definitely stirred up about Little Alfred's muddy clothes and the ring around the bathtub and being late for the relatives, who were coming for the Thanksgiving holiday.

She stormed over to the hydrant and turned off the water. Then she looked down at Little Alfred. His lower lip stuck out about two inches and he didn't look too happy about the state of the world.

"Your grandmother is going to be here any minute now, with two of your cousins, and you pick this time, of all times, to play in the mud. Just look at you!"

Little Alfred aimed his lip at her and stood on his tip-toes and said, "Dummy."

Uh oh. That was a big mistake. The boy should have kept his mouth shut. Even I could have told him that. For calling his mother a dummy, he got another swat on the behind.

He squalled, and we heard no more of that dummy business.

"Now you take those filthy clothes off right this minute and I'll have to clean you up all over again and I hope you haven't run all the water out of the pressure tank and . . ." She glanced at her watch. Her eyebrows flew straight up. "Oh my stars! They'll be here any minute!"

While Little Alfred pealed off his muddy clothes, Sally May made a dash to the water well, which was up the hill about ten yards west of the house. To get there, she had to go out the yard gate.

If you recall, I was curled up on the other side of the gate, hovering between sickness and death.

She hit that gate with a full head of steam. Maybe she didn't see me on the other side. Surely, if she'd seen me there, she wouldn't have opened the gate in such a way that it would hit me in the nose, but that's what she did.

With a wild look in her eyes, the unrollered half of her hair flying around on her head, and her housecoat sticking straight out behind her, she stepped in the middle of my back, tripped, stumbled, got up, turned back to me and screamed, "GET OUT OF THE GATE, YOU MORON, MY MOTHER-IN-LAW IS GOING TO BE HERE IN FIVE MINUTES!!"

HUH?

Well, you know me. I can take a hint. I jacked my diseased body up off the ground, moved a full six inches to the west, and collapsed again.

I wouldn't have done that for just anybody. But for Sally May, it was the least I could do.

She opened the lid on the well house, said something to the snakes and spiders and waterdogs down at the bottom, hit the reset button on the pump, and came charging back down the hill.

Halfway down the hill, she looked up and saw Little Alfred. He was standing buck-naked in the flowerbed, painting his tummy with mud and watering her flowers—without the garden hose.

"ALFRED! GET OUT OF THAT . . ."

Well, I was just lying there, minding my own business and trying to recover from the bacon poisoning. And, as I've pointed out, I had moved out of the gate, as she had requested.

Or, to put it another way, I had pretty muchly moved out of the gate. I think she could have missed me if she had been paying attention to her business.

Don't get me wrong. I'm not criticizing Sally May. Over the years, she and I have had our differences of opinion, so to speak, and our relationship has had its ups and downs—more downs than ups, I would say. But basically I'm a loyal dog. I try not to find fault with my master or his wife.

What I'm driving at is that Sally May came zooming down the hill, stepped right in the middle of my stomach, stumbled, twisted her ankle, and went crashing into the fence.

Let's get something straight before we get into the dark and bloody parts of this story. I had little or no control over the various processes of my body, which had been weakened by the toxic effects of poisoned bacon grease.

I knew, in the stillness of my heart, that this was the wrong time for my body to purge itself of the deadly poisons, and I would have gladly chosen a different time and place, had I been given a choice.

But she had stepped right in the middle of my stomach, the very part of my body which was most inflamed and uneasy.

Before I knew it, I had staggered to my feet. My head hung low and suddenly my entire body was seized by a convulsion that began in the dark pit of my stomach and moved like a wave toward the end of my nose. My head moved up and down, three times, and then . . .

Exactly how and why I threw up in her shoe, I'll never know. It wasn't my idea. As near as I can tell, her shoe had come off when she'd taken that tumble and . . .

Did I put it there? Did I ask her to stomp on my stomach? Was it my fault that the water well quit working or that Little Alfred had painted himself with mud or that her stupid kinfolks were coming for a visit? If she didn't like her stupid kinfolks . . .

No. It wasn't my fault, but guess who got blamed for everything that had ever gone wrong in the entire ten thousand years of human history.

Me.

Okay. There we were. Once I had purged the poisons from my system, I felt much better, and at that point my concern shifted from myself to Sally May. I mean, she was leaning against the fence, moaning and holding her ankle.

Hey, my master's wife was injured and what she needed was a loyal dog to lick her in the face and, you know, to give her some encouragement. That's what I had in mind when I rushed to her side.

I was in the process of reeling out my tongue to give her a nice, juicy, healing lick on the cheek when, to my complete surprise, she grabbed me around the throat and started strangling me.

"YOU HORRIBLE DOG, YOU'VE BROKEN MY LEG AND MADE MY CHILD A SAVAGE AND RUINED MY HOLIDAY, AND NOW I'M GOING TO MURDER YOU WITH MY BARE HANDS!!"

Gulk, gasp, gurgle.

Hey, she wasn't kidding. My tongue was hanging out of my mouth and my eyeballs were about to pop out of my head when, thank goodness, her mother-in-law pulled up and saved my life.

Sally May's mouth dropped open when the car came to a stop beside us. Her grip around my throat loosened. She glanced around with glazed eyes and saw herself dressed in a housecoat, one shoe on and one shoe off, half her hair up in rollers.

Her son was running wild and naked

through the yard and chasing the cat.

And her lovely little hands were around the throat of her loyal dog.

"Oh. Why, Mom, I . . . is it already eleven o'clock?"

Grandma and the two girls stared at us with big unblinking eyes. Grandma nodded her head.

Sally May removed her hands from my throat. "I was just . . . I know this must look very . . . I'm not sure I can explain . . ."

She stood up and tried to walk on her twisted ankle. She couldn't do it without limping. Her lip quivered. Her eyes filled with tears and she burst out crying.

"Oh Mom, everything's gone wrong today! The bathtub's dirty, the water well doesn't work, my baby's running around naked, I think I've broken my leg, I've ruined the holiday, and most of all, *I hate this dog*!"

Grandma came over and put her arms around Sally May. "Now, now, don't you worry about that, dearie. I've been a mother too and you don't need to explain a thing to me. After all, I was the one who raised that husband of yours."

Sally May laughed and cried at the same time and buried her face on Grandma's shoulder.

G.L. Holmes

Grandma patted her on the back, then looked down at me. I whapped my tail on the ground, just to let her know that I understood too.

She kicked me in the ribs. "Get out of here, you nasty thing! See what you've done?"

HUH?

Well, hey, if that's the way she felt about it . . . I ran for my life.

CHAPTER

6

DROVER PASSES HIS TEST, BUT JUST BARELY

Instead of running to a far corner of the ranch, as most ordinary dogs would have done once they had worn out their respective welcomes, I hid in some weeds and watched what happened next.

I mean, Sally May had injured herself, right? Even though my conscience was clear on the matter, even though she had accused me of crimes I didn't commit, I was still concerned about her. And besides that, a guy never knows when someone is going to pull out some food and leave scraps lying around. Part of my job as Head of Ranch Security is keeping the place clean.

I'm kind of a fanatic about cleanliness. Nothing trashes up a place quite as badly as trash, and if that happens to include, oh, scraps of bread, baloney rings, chicken bones, pieces of hot dog—just about any of the food groups except vegetables and things that taste or smell like bacon—then so much the better.

There's nothing wrong or selfish about combining a zeal for cleanliness with an interest in food. Without food, where would we be in this old life? We'd all be going around looking for something to eat, which brings us back to my original concern: Sally May had injured her ankle, and I was worried about her.

Also hungry. I'd lost my breakfast, right? You can't expect a dog to operate on fresh air and sunshine . . . I don't want to beat the point to death but . . . okay. Sally May dried her tears and hobbled around on her bum leg, while Grandma went into the yard, scooped up Little Alfred, and hauled him into the house for a session in the bathtub.

When they came back outside, Alfred had shed most of his mud and was wearing civilized clothes again.

Grandma shook her finger in the boy's face and told him to stay the heck out of the mud, then she went over and looked at Sally May's ankle. She poked and squeezed, squinted her eyes and pooched out her lips, and finally said,

"Hun, I think we'd better take you to town and let the doctor look at this."

Sally May let out a groan. "But why did it have to happen on the day before Thanksgiving? If I ever see that dog again . . ."

She turned around and looked in my direction. I concentrated extra hard on blending into the environment, so to speak, and was prepared to run if she reached for a rock or a gun.

I didn't mind taking the blame for crimes I didn't commit, but my idea of being a nice guy stops short of getting murdered for it.

Sally May limped inside and changed her clothes, while Grandma herded all the kids into the car. Then Sally May came out again, using a mop for a crutch. Her eyes had a certain pinched quality about them when she looked off to the south, and I had a suspicion that she hadn't entirely given up the idea of strangling . . . well, ME, you might say.

"This is so embarrassing!" she said, as she scooted into the car seat, and I didn't hear the rest because she slammed the door.

I scrunched down in the weeds and didn't move a hair until they were gone and I heard the car rumble over the cattle guard. Then I stood up and took a deep breath.

I guess I shouldn't let little things bother me, but it kind of hurt me to see Sally May taking out all her sorrows and frustrations on me.

I know that's part of my job, but sometimes it's hard to take, especially when those girls hadn't left a single food scrap on the ground. I know because I went over the whole area three times. Not even a crumb. Sure was hungry. Sure could have used a crumb or a pound of hamburger.

Pete the Plow was sitting in the sun, licking his coat and trying to recover his dignity. Just for laughs, I hollered at him, asked how he'd enjoyed babysitting with Sally May's little monster.

He didn't answer, which was fine because I had better things to do than listen to a half-drownded cat.

I went down to the gas tanks and found Drover, standing with his nose pressed against the northeast angle-iron leg of the gas tanks. He was mumbling something.

"All right, son, it's examination time. I presume you've been studying your lessons?"

"Sure have, Hank, and I'm bored."

"Don't worry about it. Anybody who had spent the last half-hour with you would have been bored."

"So it's not just me?"

"Not at all. It's a perfectly natural reaction. But let me remind you, Drover, that this was punishment. I didn't send you down here to be frivolous."

"What does 'frillivous' mean?"

"The word is *frivolous,* and it means silly, unbusinesslike, unprofessional, greedy, self-centered, disrespectful, discourteous, disobedient, irreverent, and basically stupid."

"Gosh, that's quite a word."

"Indeed it is, and it wouldn't hurt you to remember it."

"Yeah, and then I wouldn't forget it."

"Exactly. I think you'll find, Drover, that a few fancy words, sprinkled here and there into your sentences, would help break the monogamy of your conversation."

"Gosh. What happens when you break your mahogany?"

"You either fix it or it stays broke."

"Don't they paint mahogany sometimes?"

"Sometimes they do, but plywood is much cheaper. How did we get on the subject of plywood?"

"I don't know. We were talking about big words."

"Yes, that's true. Plywood is a big word,

Drover, and you should try to sprinkle it into your conversation more often. Who knows, you might fool someone."

"Okay. You seen any plywood this morning?"

"Why do you ask?"

"Just trying to fool you."

I couldn't help chuckling at that. "Drover, if you really and truly want to fool Hank the Cowdog, you should bring camping gear, because it could take you weeks or even months. Now, where were we?"

"Plywood."

"Exactly. Plywood. Hmmm. I seem to have lost my train of thought."

"Can I take my nose out of the corner now?"

"Negative, unless you can pass a very thorough and difficult examination, and I have my doubts about that."

"Oh gosh. I've got a crick in my neck from holding my nose in the corner."

"I'm sorry to hear that, Drover, but I hope you understand that crickets have no bearing on this case. It doesn't matter how many crickets you've seen, or think you've seen. No amount of crickets can excuse your behavior."